FORBIDDEN VAMPIRE MATE

MATCHMATER PARANORMAL DATING APP #3

LAURA GREENWOOD

Nothing is more forbidden than a bite...

The first time she uses the MatchMater App, Effie finds the one person she can't have. Forbidden from mating with anyone who isn't a faerie, she has to go against every belief her people have if she wants a chance at happiness.

Wendell isn't one for tradition, and he couldn't care less what his mate's people say. He is going to prove to her that the forbidden fruit is often the most delicious.

Forbidden Vampire Mate is book 3 in the MatchMater Paranormal Dating App series. It is Effie and Wendell's complete romance.

CHAPTER ONE

WENDELL

WENDELL SIGHED and rubbed a hand over his face as he studied the brief in front of him. It was dull reading, but he had to do it if he wanted to get the promotion at the end of the year. Perhaps he should have listened to his mother when she suggested he worked in a vampire focused firm, instead of one that worked with humans too.

Most of the time, he didn't mind. He liked it when he could help people with their problems, especially when it looked bleak for them. But the firm was going through a dry spell when it came to interesting cases.

The door to his office cracked open.

He looked up and groaned inwardly at the sight of a blonde-haired woman he knew only too well.

"What do you want, Cora?" he asked, hoping she'd tell him and then disappear to go do whatever it was she did.

Instead, she took it as an invitation into his space.

He sighed and shut the folder, not wanting her to see what he'd been working on. It wasn't that he didn't trust her...actually, it was. Cora was one of the least reliable people he'd ever met. As well as one of the most cunning. She didn't even work in his building, and yet had managed to get past the front desk.

Again. He'd have to talk to them about that, though it likely wasn't their fault. She'd probably used some kind of compulsion on them. She'd never told him whether or not she could use the vampire specific skill, but he'd always assumed so.

"What do you want?" he asked again when she stayed quiet.

Cora hopped up onto his desk and crossed her legs, letting her skirt ride up higher than she should and reveal her stockings.

He looked away and sighed. Gone were the days when showing an ankle was frowned upon. Where Cora was concerned, he wanted them back.

"Can't I just come say hello?" she purred.

"I've told you, we're not together," he pointed out.

She leaned in and took his tie in her hand, giving it a gentle tug so he came closer. "We're mates, Wendell, you can't deny it."

He pulled his tie away from her, and tucked it back into place before leaning back in his chair. "How many times do I have to tell you, we're not mates, Cora. We spent one night together a couple of decades ago."

"And yet you haven't been able to stay away from me since."

Wendell took a deep breath. How had she not got it all through her head yet? He'd done everything he could in the past twenty-or-so years to separate the two of them, including moving to a completely new town to be away from her. It hadn't worked for long. She'd found him after only two years.

Unfortunately for him, he'd fallen in love with the town during that time, and didn't want to leave. He loved the laid back feel of it, as well as walking down the paths next to the estuary, the smell of the sea in the air, and the breeze rushing past him. He'd lived in big cities his entire life, like most vampires, this was a nice change of pace.

Cora grabbed his phone from the desk before he had a chance to stop her. He should have thought about and moved it away the moment she stepped into the room. He never learned fast enough where she was concerned.

"What's this?" she hissed, jabbing a finger at the screen.

"I don't know. You tell me." He shrugged. It was hard to tell what she was annoyed about if he couldn't see it.

"Why have you downloaded this?"

His mind raced through all the things he'd downloaded to his phone, but he couldn't come up with a single thing that could have triggered her. Of course, that didn't mean anything as far as Cora was concerned. She was a loose cannon, and one he was ready to be rid of.

"MatchMater." Venom dripped from the single word.

Oh. That would explain her annoyance.

"My friend recommended it, I thought I'd try it."

"And what about me?" Anger flared in her eyes.

"You're *not* my mate, Cora. We'd know about it by now." This was getting tiring. He didn't know how many times he could have the same conversation with her and still maintain his patience.

"You should give us a chance..."

He groaned. When would she understand all of this? Maybe he should put *her* on MatchMater. He dismissed the thought as soon as it came to him. He couldn't do anything without her permission. He'd just have to hope she made the decision on her own.

"Cora, it's *not* going to happen," he said firmly. "I know you think you feel some kind of mating bond with me, but I don't feel it back, and we'd know about it by now."

She pouted as she shifted on the desk, giving him another flash of leg as she did.

"We could have so much fun together, Wendell," she promised, her voice dropping low as she did.

He knew she was trying to turn him on, but she did nothing for him any more. One of the many reasons he knew they weren't mates.

"I'm sorry, Cora. I have a lot of work to do. Can we do this later?" It was the only thing he could think of to get her out of his office. It was almost as bad as when he had to go somewhere he knew she'd be.

"But Wendell..." She eyed him as if she was about to strip him and have her way with him. He wished she wouldn't.

"Go. Cora." He gave her the sternest look he could manage, though he doubted it would be enough to put her off. He truly didn't understand what her obsession with him was. There'd been nothing noteworthy about their night together. At least, not that he could remember. He'd made no promises to her, and nor had she to him. That was how it had to be with other paranormals. Unless all the parties involved were mates, nothing serious could ever happen. It was as simple as that.

She looked as if she was going to argue, but then decided against it.

Relief flooded through him as Cora slunk off out of his office, leaving him alone and able to focus again. He turned back to his computer and pulled up his list of meetings. If he was lucky, he had time to grab a coffee before the next one.

But not before he sent a message to Jim. The incubus had gotten him into this predicament by recommending that he got MatchMater in the first place, he could help get him out of it by figuring out how to ditch Cora once and for all too.

CHAPTER TWO

*E*FFIE

EFFIE DIMMED THE LIGHTS, setting the ambience for something more soothing than the harsh light the nursing home gave them. The door creaked open as her two o'clock stepped in.

"Hello, dear."

Effie gulped. Something always felt a little off about this woman, no matter how many times she treated her.

"Good afternoon. Same as usual?" she asked.

"Yes, dear. That sounds good. But be careful around the wing area."

She stiffened. "The wing area?" She hoped the

woman meant bingo wings and wasn't trying to insinuate that she knew something about what Effie was. That wouldn't go down very well with the rest of the Faerie Council.

The woman gave her a knowing look. "Do you really need me to say it out loud?"

"I find that communication is always the best way to ensure a positive customer experience." Her voice waved as she spoke, but she knew it had to be said. Dealing with her very human boss would be even worse than dealing with the Faerie Council.

"I'm just asking as one-winged being to another, that you be careful around the delicate area. Though I do have to say, you're much better at that than the other one." The woman sat down on the massage chair.

"Winged being?" she squeaked, while still going through the routines of a normal massage. She wouldn't have anyone say that she was bad at her job. Even when she was surprised by conversations like this one, she was determined to do the right thing and see the appointment through.

"Please, you're leaving pixie dust everywhere," the woman pointed out.

"Faerie," Effie muttered under her breath without thinking.

The woman chuckled. "That's the quickest way I know of getting a faerie to admit what they are."

"How did you know?" There was no point denying it at this point, not when the woman had already worked it out.

"I've been around a long time. There are few things I haven't seen in my time, and faeries are included in that."

"But how? We only came out of hiding five years ago." Most faeries hadn't even moved out into the human world yet. They were too scared of the consequences. Mostly due to stories like the one about the boy dressed in green who used faerie dust to fly.

"I lived on the other side of the portal while the faerie still lived with the fae. Nasty split, that." She shook her head, seeming genuinely sorry for the situation.

"But...how?"

"Please, you can't be naive enough to not know that paranormals are long-lived. That wasn't even half my life ago."

Effie's eyes widened at the thought. Living so long wasn't something most faeries experienced. Mostly due to boredom and stupid mistakes. A lot of faeries would dare one another to do dangerous things, and often would end up hurting themselves beyond repair.

"Are you on MatchMater yet?" the woman asked.

"MatchMater? What's that?" Effie frowned, trying to work out what that could mean.

"It's an app. You have a phone, I assume?" The woman held out her hand, clearly expecting Effie to just hand it over. "Don't worry, it's been approved by the High Council. You won't be breaking any laws by using it."

Effie couldn't see a way to argue with that. Not when the woman seemed to know so much about her from the little they'd interacted. And without revealing some of the intricacies of faerie politics, she couldn't say no.

She restrained a sigh as she handed her phone to the old woman. Perhaps it wasn't her best idea, but something deep within her was telling her she should go ahead and do it. That this would lead to something good for her.

Even if it wasn't what the Faerie Council had in mind for its people. She didn't imagine there were many faerie men on the app, and even if there were, she'd probably already met them and dismissed them as not her mate.

"There are some yummy looking men on here," Mrs Stein mused as she clicked on buttons, doing...*something*. Effie didn't pretend to understand half of the things her phone was capable of doing. She only used it to communicate with the people she worked with. They'd found it odd that she didn't have a phone when she first started her training.

"I'm sure there are," Effie agreed, though she wasn't sure why. She shouldn't be encouraging the old woman. Even if a part of her did want to meet her mate, the rest could only think about the ban on inter-species mating from the Faerie Council.

It was a complex ruling that she didn't really understand. Apparently, if someone found their true mate, then it would be accepted, but faeries were banned from *looking* if it wasn't within the faery community. She wasn't sure what the punishment for it was, though. No one did. As teenagers, they'd whispered about banishment, but there hadn't been anyone with the predicament during her life, which made it difficult to be sure.

"Oh, he's nice. I have a good feeling about this one," Mrs Stein said, pulling Effie back from her thoughts. "I should swipe him for you..."

"No," Effie half-shouted, before remembering where she was and who she was talking to. If she lost this job, then she doubted her parents would let her leave the faery realm for work. She knew she shouldn't be letting them rule her life now she was in

11

her twenties, but for a lot of the older faeries, it was a given that children followed their parents rules for their entire lives.

Mrs Stein chuckled and handed Effie's phone back. "I'm sorry, dear. I shouldn't have pried so far. But seeing my grandson happily mated has made me think I'm a bit of a matchmaker." She smiled reassuringly.

"No, I'm sorry, Mrs Stein. I forgot where I was, and that isn't acceptable." She slipped her phone back in her pocket. Perhaps she should delete the app first, but a small part of her didn't want to. There was something exciting about it.

Forbidden, even.

The rest of her day passed in a blur of patients and thoughts of what she was going to do about the app on her phone. She shouldn't be thinking about it. She should delete it and have done with it all. Nothing good could come from using it. She'd end up either heartbroken, or expelled from her people, neither of which sounded particularly fun if she was honest with herself.

And yet, she was resistant to press uninstall. Actually, if she was honest with herself, she wanted to *use* it. There were worst things she could do than look for her mate under the radar. She left the faery realm all the time, which meant she *could* meet someone that way. And if any of her people asked, then that's what she'd say. No. That was what she'd have to say.

Effie sighed as she tidied up the room she'd been using for the day. The decision could wait until tomorrow. One day on the app wouldn't hurt.

CHAPTER THREE

WENDELL

HIS FLAT WAS DEATHLY STILL when he returned for the evening. Wendell sighed and made his way through the rooms, checking for Cora. It wouldn't be the first time she'd broken into his flat and waited for him. He was fairly certain she had a key made. Not that something as flimsy as a lock would stop her. He wasn't sure how she did it, but Cora was a mastermind when it came to getting in places. If she put half the energy she spent on Wendell on something else, she could build a career for herself.

Satisfied the female vampire wasn't lying in wait for him, he made his way to the kitchen. It had been a long day at the office despite the lack of interesting cases, and he hadn't managed to eat anything since lunch.

He pottered around the small room, making a cup of tea while he waited for the oven to heat up so he could put a ready-made lasagna in. His Mum would be disappointed if she knew how much he relied on ready meals, but there was no way around it sometime. If he had someone else to share his life with, then perhaps it would be different. He did enjoy cooking, having learned from his Mum when he was still a boy.

With a sigh, he pulled open the fridge for some milk, spying his blood pouches in the process. His stomach growled with a different kind of hunger. He counted back the days since he'd last had blood, but lost count. Had it really been that long? His blood subscription arrived every two weeks, no matter how much he drank, so that wasn't anything to go by. The older he got, the less often he had to drink. It was a common thing that happened with vampires, and one that made them a lot less cool than human fiction made them out to be. He suspected that a lot of humans would be disappointed to learn the truth about his species.

All of that paled into insignificance considering how much he needed to drink now. He grabbed the blood pouch along with the milk. After milking his tea, he set the bottle down and turned his attention to the blood. Within a few moments, he had the top of the bag open, and the blood sloshing into the mug. He wasn't sure what they did to it before they delivered it to vampires like him, but it was thinner than straight from the vein, and also tastier. He suspected the company added something to it to make it last longer. After Wendell had been introduced to it by a friend, he'd never turned back. Drinking from humans was messy to say the least, and if they'd eaten the wrong thing, then it could taste bad. This way, at least he knew what he was putting into his body in advance.

He shoved the mug in the microwave and heated it for thirty seconds. He didn't always do that, but it *was* better warm.

With his tea and his blood in hand, he left the kitchen and made his way into the living room of his flat. It wasn't a huge place, he didn't need much space for just him, but it was more spacious than the one he'd had in London, and half the price.

He set down his mugs and flicked on the TV. He loaded up one of his favourite property buying shows, and leaned back, making himself comfortable. His life would be so much better if he had someone to share it with. Someone who *wasn't* Cora. Though he'd lived through this many years without finding his mate, he had to wonder how many more it would be. That was one of the downsides of being a vampire. They lived so long that it could be hundreds of years before their mate was even born, particularly if that person started out as human.

He pulled out his phone and tapped on the red M of the MatchMater app. It couldn't hurt to look through the women on there. If he was lucky, he'd find the *one*. If he was unlucky, he wouldn't have lost anything other than a little bit of time. It was certainly worth a shot, and he had time to kill before his lasagna was ready anyway.

With a swig of blood for courage, he flicked through the first few women. It was great knowing the High Council approved the app, and that everyone on it was who they said they were. He wasn't completely sure how they did that, but sometimes it was better not to know. Nothing about the first three women called to him. Was he doing it wrong? Should he be basing it off their looks instead of the gut feeling he had about them? He should have asked Jim about it more before starting.

All the doubts fled from his mind as the sixth woman appeared on his screen. She was breathtaking, but it wasn't anything to do with her looks. Though with her big brown eyes and thick flowing hair would count her as that. It was something more than that. She was magical. The tug in his gut was impossible to ignore. This woman was someone he had to talk to. He needed to be near her, and learn more about her.

He glanced at the name.

Effie.

Her species was hidden, but he didn't care. She was a paranormal, which meant the pull he was feeling was real. He didn't care what she was, or what kind of magic she was using to put a spell on him. It was probably nothing at all.

"Effie," he said her name out loud, loving the way it sounded.

Perfect. Every part of her.

He shook his head. How was he thinking this way about a woman he'd never even met? This wasn't like him. He was logical, thoughtful, and slow to make decisions.

And yet he found himself swiping yes on the woman who just felt right. A warm contented feeling washed over him, and he shut off the app. Perhaps that was the wrong when he'd only found one potential match, but it felt like the right thing to do, and that was enough for him.

CHAPTER FOUR

EFFIE

EFFIE'S PHONE vibrated in her pocket, but only one buzz. It must be a message rather than a call. She frowned, trying to work out who could be messaging her. The only people who ever contacted her were work and her parents, both of whom preferred to call.

She glanced over her shoulder to check her Mum wasn't looking. It wasn't that she was *hiding* anything from the older woman per-say, but it was better if she checked these things without a pair of eagle eyes over her shoulder.

The screen lit up, revealing a small M icon at the top. Her eyes widened. Had she found a match on

MatchMater already? She hadn't even swiped for anyone. Unless...

No. Mrs Stein wouldn't have done that, would she? The woman clearly thought of herself as a bit of a matchmaker, but that didn't mean she'd do anything as dangerous as trying to match for Effie.

"Euphemia, are you there?" her Mum called.

She winced at the use of her full name. She hated it, and insisted on people using Effie instead. Her Mum was the only person who didn't seem to care about what she wanted to be called and continued to use it.

"Yes," she answered, then shut off her phone and returned it to her pocket.

She made her way into the next room, which her Mum used as an office. Though she didn't actually work, so Effie didn't know what the point of the room was.

"Did you need me for something?" Effie asked, her only thoughts surrounding when she could be alone to look at the match she'd made. While she didn't like the idea of someone else doing it for her, she was intrigued by what the app might have come up with.

"Your wings aren't out," her Mum said.

"Oh, I must have forgotten when I came back through the veil." She focused on her back and expanded her wings outwards. A warm fuzzy feeling fell over her as the wings broke out, filling the space behind her. She sighed, loving them being free. Hiding them was the only disadvantage of spending some of her time in the human world. But it was a price she was willing to pay for the freedom it brought her.

Her Mum's face grew serious. Effie steeled herself for what she knew was coming. They had the same conversation at least once every couple of weeks, and she could probably have recited it without her Mum even being in the room.

"I don't know why you keep going to the human realm."

"Because I have a job," Effie replied. There was no other way of explaining it. If she'd said it was to do with her personal freedom, then her Mum wouldn't accept it. She thought faeries had it the best of all the paranormals in their sheltered world.

It wasn't technically a different realm like the one the fae lived in, but it was separated from the human one. No one but faeries, and those who already knew where it was could find it. Which was a source of great comfort to a lot of the older faeries, and boredom to the younger ones. Effie was far from the only one in her generation who had gotten a job in the human world. Though there were so few of them in total that most paranormals probably had no idea that the faeries even still existed.

"You don't need a job. You should stay here and settle down with a nice faery..."

"How am I going to settle down with someone I don't love?" Effie responded. "You're lucky you found Dad. You know most of us don't find our mates within the faery race. It's one of the reasons we're dying out." The instant the words were out of her mouth, she regretted them. It wasn't her Mum's fault that the Faerie Council were so short sighted and didn't allow faeries to mix with other races.

Her Mum pursed her lips. "Perhaps if you spent more of your time at our gatherings, or visiting the other faery villages, you'd find someone to your liking."

Effie closed her eyes and counted to five, trying to keep her composure as much as she could. She loved her parents, but they could be so short sighted sometimes. "It's not about finding someone I can settle for. It's about finding the perfect match for me. And if I want kids, then I'm going to *have* to find my actual mate, not just someone who'll do." Which what a lot of faeries had done. It was proving disastrous for their numbers, as only mated couples could have children.

When the heavy silence between the two women grew too much to bear, Effie sighed.

"Let's not get into this now," she said, knowing neither of them were going to change their opinions on the matter. It was pointless rehashing the same thing over and over again and expecting a different result.

"Fine. Your Dad will be home with dinner in a couple of hours." Her Mum sounded resigned but not annoyed, which was a good sign.

"I'll be back down for then," Effie promised, before slipping out of the room and into the hall with a high ceiling.

She opened her wings and flapped them slightly, readying herself to take off. This was one of the best parts about living in the faery village, and she found that stairs could be a bit tedious at times when out in the human world. Effie launched herself into the air and flew up a few stories until she came to her bedroom door. She hovered in front of it, using the delicate wings she'd been born with to hold herself steady. She reached out and let herself into the room that had been hers since she'd learned to fly.

Effie dumped her bag on the desk and pulled her phone out, too intrigued by the MatchMater notification to put off looking at it. She flopped onto her bed and pressed it.

Her screen flashed, taking her straight to the profile of a handsome man with dirty blond hair.

Wendell, vampire.

An odd feeling swept over her, urging her to do more than just look at him. She wished he was in the room with her, that the two of them could talk and spend time together. Or perhaps do something more than that. It had been a long time since she'd spent the night with one of the other faeries her age. Around the same amount of time she'd been longing for more.

Her finger hovered over the message button. Should she press it? She knew she shouldn't. Faerie law forbid it. But that didn't stop her from wanting it.

She had to.

Besides, who would know she'd done it? If the Faerie Council were monitoring the app, then they already knew she'd signed up to it, and nothing bad had happened.

No one would know if she messaged this Wendell. It would almost be rude not to, considering they'd matched. Plus, she hadn't been the one who did the swiping,

She touched the button before she could talk herself out of it, then typed and hit enter.

Hi.

The word stared at her. She almost couldn't believe she'd actually done it, but the excitement travelling through her entire body was too much to ignore. She'd done the right thing, she was certain of it,

Besides, there was no going back now.

CHAPTER FIVE

WENDELL

HE HATED everyone who had ever told him that love put a spring in people's steps, but only because they were right. Maybe it was too soon for him to be thinking about love, but the conversation he'd had the night before with Effie had spoken to him in ways he'd never experienced with anyone before. If he'd been on the fence about what Cora meant to him, then this would certainly have sorted it out. She was nothing more than a mistake he made twenty years ago. He felt bad for her at times. She was a nice enough person if he ignored the odd obsession.

"Good afternoon, sir. Is it a table for one?" the maitre d' asked.

Wendell shook his head. "I'm meeting a friend." He spotted Jim already at a table and waved his greeting.

"Excellent. Do you have a jacket you'd like me to check?"

"No, thank you."

With the maitre d' satisfied, Wendell made his way over to his friend and dropped himself into the seat opposite.

"Is there a reason you look like a cat who got the cream?" Jim asked, taking a long sip of his water.

"I don't look like that."

Jim raised an eyebrow. "You're forgetting you're talking to an incubus. I can sense love and lust."

"Damn." Why did he have to have perceptive friends?

The other man chuckled. "So, what happened?"

"I used MatchMater like you suggested," he admitted. "I don't know why I waited so long. I should have tried it long ago."

Jim smiled and nodded. "Or you used it at just the right time. I swear, sometimes it feels as if the app knows when we're ready to use it and when we aren't."

"That sounds about right," Wendell muttered.

"I take it you already matched with someone you like?" The incubus didn't phrase it like a question.

Probably because he could sense the answer just by sitting and doing his incubus-y thing.

"Yes," Wendell said. "I didn't think it would happen so fast. But a couple of people in and I knew she was the one I want to talk to. There was something about her..." He trailed off as the image of Effie's wide brown eyes swam through his mind.

It was strange how captivated he was by someone he'd never met, and yet, it felt so natural. This was the future of mating, there was no doubt in his mind.

"What is she?" Jim asked.

"Can I take your order?" a young waitress asked, cutting between their conversation.

"The house burger, please," Jim replied.

"Two, please," Wendell added. He hadn't looked at the menu yet, but he didn't need to. Whenever he met Jim for lunch during the week, they came here. He could probably recite it by heart. "And a sparkling water, please. Lemon but no ice."

"Got it. That'll be right with you," the waitress said, disappearing as suddenly as she arrived.

Wendell turned back to his companion, reminding himself that they were talking about Effie. He pulled his phone out and clicked on the app so he could show Jim a photo.

"I can show you a picture, but I don't know what kind of paranormal she is. It felt rude to ask." He turned his phone so the other man could see. Something he was only doing because the incubus was happily mated with a woman of his own thanks to MatchMater. He had no reason to worry about the incubus magic accidentally being triggered. Though Jim wasn't the type for that.

"Ah." Recognition filled Jim's voice.

Did he already know the woman on the screen? Wendell had known Jim for a long time, and couldn't recall ever having run into her. Perhaps she was one of Rosie's friends. The siren had only just met Jim, so her friends would be brand new to him.

"One of the nurses at work needs some legal advice, would you be able to come down later this afternoon?" Jim asked.

Wendell frowned, wondering what the change of subject was all about. But he trusted his friend, and that he had a good reason for suggesting it. Perhaps he needed some time to figure out why he recognised Effie and to do something about it? Whatever the explanation, Wendell decided it was better if he went with it.

"Sure. I have some casework to catch up on, but I can log some pro-bono hours after that and come down."

Jim nodded. "Thanks, I know she'll really appreciate it. She's found herself in a bit of a sticky situation."

Their food arrived before they could talk about it more, and they changed the subject to catch up on the local rugby scores. It wasn't something that interested either of them massively, but the point of these lunches was to have a break and some easy conversation away from their lives.

"I need some help with Cora," Wendell said as he pushed his plate away. He couldn't believe he'd almost forgotten about the most important thing he wanted to ask his friend about. "She's still convinced that we're mates. And it could be a problem now."

"Because it wasn't before?" Jim teased.

"You have a point there. But before, it was only me she might have scared off. Now I'm looking at a potential mate too, it's not good at all. And I don't want to hurt Cora either. Obsession aside, she's a good person, I think."

"Hmm. That is a tricky one. Especially as I guess you've already tried simply telling her you're not mates."

"More times than I want to count," Wendell admitted glumly. "I'm not sure what it is that convinces her we are. There was nothing special about *that* night." If he remembered it right, he'd let the alcohol affect him, which had been one of the reasons he'd ended up in bed with Cora to begin with. She was a beautiful woman, after all.

"I suppose using the new girl to do it is too harsh..." Jim started to suggest.

Wendell groaned. "Let's pretend for now that isn't even an option."

"It might be the only one that gets through to her."

"I hope you're wrong. Is there some kind of reward for signing up to MatchMater? Maybe if I can convince her to do that, then she'll forget about me." He was clutching at straws, and he knew it, but it was better than nothing. It had to be.

"I don't think so. And we can't sign her up without her knowing," Jim said, echoing Wendell's thought from before.

He sighed deeply. "There's just no getting around it, is there?" The question didn't need an answer. He already knew it. Until he convinced Cora that there was nothing between them, he was stuck with her in his life.

"I'm sorry I can't be more help." At least the incubus seemed sincere about that.

"What time do you want me to come to the nursing home?" Wendell asked his friend.

Jim shrugged. "Whatever time suits. If you text

me when you're setting off, then I'll make sure the nurse is on her break."

Wendell narrowed his eyes. What was he up to? He hadn't said the woman's name at any point during the conversation, which was weird enough as it was.

"Will do." He had a feeling about this. Not a bad one, but something he couldn't shake. Going to Jim's place of work was important, and that was about all he was certain of right now.

CHAPTER SIX

Effie

Effie tucked a strand of loose hair behind her ear. Really, she should retie it completely, but she was too distracted with playing the conversation from last night over and over in her head. She'd felt a deep connection to the person on the other end of the phone, despite not being able to see his face or hear his voice.

She needed to pull herself together and stop thinking about it. At this rate, she was going to lose her job by not paying enough attention. She was probably only feeling a rush of adrenaline from using the MatchMater app for the first time and talking to someone she hadn't known for most of her life. That didn't mean it was anything special, nor that it was going to lead to more.

The driveway up to the nursing home was surprisingly empty for a lunchtime. Often the residents' families would visit during this time. At least, the ones who worked close enough would.

Effie enjoyed the slight breeze through her hair as she walked under the trees. It was a beautiful place for the people here to live out the rest of their days. The grounds were well kept, with an assortment of trees, flowers, and other plants, as well as plenty to do inside. A lot of the people here seemed happy from what they said to Effie when they visited her treatment room.

The entrance appeared faster than she wanted it to. She had a full set of appointments this afternoon. Which was fine, really. She loved her job, and the fact she could infuse her patients with a little bit of magic to take away the ache of their ageing bodies. It was one of the reasons she'd opted for a nursing home instead of working in a beauty parlour. Well, that and the fact a lot of human women in their twenties and thirties were a little hostile towards her. She was fairly certain it was because of the faery aura she gave off.

While faeries weren't the same as fae, they had some similar characteristics, and an ethereal glow was one of them. Effie simply wished she was able to turn it off sometimes. She didn't want people to hate her for no real reason.

She was so lost in thought, she forgot to watch where she was going. Within moments, she ran straight into the chest of someone.

Shock rushed through her system, along with something else she couldn't put a name to. She pushed it to the side and stepped back.

"I'm so sorry," she said while brushing herself off. "I don't normally walk into strangers," she promised.

When she looked up a moment later, she sucked in a breath. The man standing in front of her wasn't a stranger at all.

Kind of.

"I'll get back to work," a second man said.

She glanced in his direction and frowned. She knew him. Jim. One of the doctors. He smiled at her, then disappeared.

"Hi," she squeaked.

"Effie, isn't it?" Wendell asked, a knowing smile on his face. "I knew he was up to something."

"Who?" she asked, forgetting he'd checked her name. He knew who she was, she could see it in his eyes.

"Jim. He's been planning something since I told him about you at lunch."

"You told him about me?" she squeaked.

He nodded. "Maybe about two hours ago. He said he'd make sure you were on a break when I arrived."

She frowned. "I haven't spoken to Jim today. How did he know I was on a late lunch?" It was nearing half-past three already. She'd done what she normally did and planned her lunch around her appointments.

"He probably didn't. I think that's my fault actually. I turned up earlier than he expected me to."

"He told you to come meet me?" A small thrill ran through her at that, even though she knew it shouldn't. She needed to remember how dangerous this could be for her, and not just her heart either.

What was she getting herself into?

"No. He tricked me. Kind of." Wendell pushed a hand through his dirty blond hair.

She bit her lip, trying not to think about how much more attractive she found him in person. It wasn't simply the way he looked, it was more than that. Like the very way he stood and just was.

"He told me a nurse needed some legal advice after he saw your picture." He frowned. "Unless he was telling the truth..."

She chuckled. "Sorry, he wasn't. I'm neither a nurse, or in need of legal advice. You've had a wasted trip, I'm afraid."

"Far from it."

His voice rumbled through her. Beneath the skin of her back, her wings tried to quiver, a sensation she'd never felt before. What had caused it? This man, or the danger? Conflicted thoughts continued to run through her head. This was only going to make the rest of her day go even slower.

"While you're here, would you like to go on a proper date with me, rather than a meet-cute set up by an incubus?" he asked.

Every part of her wanted to scream yes, that there was nothing she wanted more. Time with him would be time well spent. But despite that, she knew she couldn't. As hard as it was, she had to respect the laws her people had put in place. That was her job as one of them. She *had* to obey, no matter how hard it was, or how much she wanted Wendell.

She took a deep breath, ignoring her entire body shaking. It was impossible not to let it get to her.

"I'm sorry. I can't."

She didn't wait for him to say anything. She couldn't. If he had a chance to speak to her, then he'd convince her that it was a good idea for the two of them to go out together, and she couldn't afford that, no matter what he said.

For what felt like the first time, the twisty hallways of the nursing home played into her hands. She knew them well enough that she wasn't going to get lost, but Wendell wouldn't.

Her heart broke with every step she took, but she knew it was for the best. She'd already fallen further than she should have let herself.

CHAPTER SEVEN

WENDELL

HE PUSHED AWAY the mounting pile of work, unable to focus on any of it after his disastrous attempt at asking Effie out on a date. What confused him the most was the connection he'd felt between them. He'd never experienced anything like it before, unless he counted the initial one when they'd made contact for the first time, but somehow, it didn't compare.

They'd already connected while they were talking, and now they'd met in person, something had snapped into place. He didn't need it spelling out for him, though he'd heard rumours that the Match-Mater app *would* do that at some point. After today's reaction to a mere date, he suspected that Effie wasn't ready to hit the mated button yet, even if it was clearly the way they should be going.

The phone rang, and he jumped to answer it, hoping against all odds, that it was Effie. It was silly to think so, considering it was his work line and he hadn't given her his number.

"Hello, Wendell speaking, how can I help?" he asked as he placed the receiver by his ear.

"So, how did it go?"

His heart sank at the sound of Jim's voice, which wasn't the usual reaction he had to his oldest friend calling.

"She ran away."

"That good, eh?" The incubus chuckled down the line. "What did you do?"

"Asked her out on a date," he admitted, pushing a hand through his hair. No doubt he'd done that enough times to make it stick up on end by now.

"Ouch." The line crackled.

"Yes, ouch. What am I going to do?"

"Give her time," Jim suggested. "One of Rosie's friends had a mate who wouldn't accept things at first. He came around in the end, you just have to give it time."

Wendell sighed. "I figured as much. I thought I'd send her a message so she knows I'm still interested

44

in the date when she is. Hopefully, she won't take too long to come around, or I'm going to go crazy."

Jim chuckled down the phone. "That sounds about right. I didn't want to spend much time away from Rosie when we first met. The pull was far too strong. You should be reassured by that. Your girl will come around to it."

"I don't want to force her into anything she doesn't want," Wendell admitted softly. It wasn't what a lot of paranormals would want to hear, but it was true. Whether they were true mates or not, he wanted to give Effie what she *wanted*, not what he thought they should have.

To his surprise, Jim didn't immediately tell him he was going crazy.

"Message her," the incubus said eventually. "Once the two of you are talking, you can work out what you want from your mating. Until then, there's no point dwelling on it too much. Simply do what you can. And for water's sake, don't do what Cora does to her."

"For water's sake?" Wendell raised an eyebrow, even though his friend couldn't see him.

"Sorry, living with a siren seems to be rubbing off on me." He laughed, but turned serious almost instantly. "Message her, but don't stalk her entire life. Write what you need to say, hit send, and then close the app until she replies. No obsessing over her. And no being creepy."

"Don't worry, I promise not to go all Cora on the poor girl."

"Good. Now, I have to go. I have another patient coming in." Jim hung up the phone without another word.

Wendell sighed loudly and placed his own receiver back in the cradle. There was nothing for it. He was going to have to do exactly what Jim had suggested.

For whatever reason, Effie hadn't been ready to give their mating bond a chance to grow. Hopefully, that was merely a temporary issue, and she'd tell him they could go on a date within the next week. Now he'd found her, he didn't want to waste a moment spending time without her. It was rare enough for paranormals to find their mates still.

He grabbed his mobile and swiped straight onto the MatchMater app. Her face was right there, staring up at him with a smile in her eyes. She truly was the most exquisite creature he'd ever laid eyes on, though she'd been taller than he'd expected for some reason. All of that paled in comparison to their talk, though.

He opened up the chat and re-read some of the messages from the past couple of days.

Effie: What's your favourite book?

Wendell: Birdsong

Effie: Sebastian Faulks? Really? Is that the book you chose in order to impress women?

Wendell: Definitely not. If I wanted to do that, I'd say Sense and Sensibility. Or Emma.

Effie: Interesting choices, I'm more of a Dracula girl myself.

Wendell: Is that the book you chose in order to impress vampires?

He'd been able to imagine her smiling as she typed. He wasn't sure *how* he knew that was what she'd been doing, but the memory was entrenched along with the words.

Effie: Oh, definitely. I've only ever read it once. I can barely remember it. But you never said. Why Birdsong?

Wendell: The imagery and the emotions it invokes. I truly feel as if I'm transported when I read it. I know that sounds strange, but it's the truth.

Effie: I get it. I felt that way about Private Peaceful too.

Wendell: Morpurgo? Interesting choice.

Effie: It's a modern classic. The Butterfly Lion too. You won't change my mind.

Wendell: I wasn't planning on. It is *a modern classic. Though I haven't read the second one you mentioned. I'll have to download it so I can listen to it at work.*

And he had done. She was right, it as another modern classic. He couldn't wait to be able to properly talk to her about it when they finally got to go on a date.

He scrolled past the rest of their chat. Everything from food, to music. Their tastes had lined up a lot, though it shone through that she was a little younger than he was. That didn't matter, though. They'd have a long life together to explore everything they both liked.

But that didn't solve the problem he was faced with now. How was he going to convince her to date him without being unnecessarily pushy?

Wendell: Hi, Effie, it was nice to see you today, I'm sorry I took you by surprise, I didn't mean to freak you out. If you want to go on a proper date, just the two of us (I'll leave the meddling incubus at home) then let me know. I'm willing to wait as long as you need me to.

He stared at it for a long moment, deleting parts and re-adding them until he was happy. There was so much more he wanted to say, but he knew he had to be careful if he wanted her to say yes to a date. This was a long game, and he was willing to play it for as long as he needed to.

CHAPTER EIGHT

EFFIE

SHE SHOULD REALLY THINK about uninstalling the MatchMater app. The little M notification was burning a hole in her metaphorical pocket. She'd seen it pop up and knew it had to be Wendell sending her some kind of message. No doubt it would be a sweet one, asking her out on another date she wanted to say yes to.

A knock sounded on the door.

"Come in," she called. Her next patient was due any moment, and it was likely to be them.

To her surprise, Mrs Stein skipped into the room, not even bothering to hide that she wasn't as elderly as she was pretending to be. Actually, that was wrong. She was probably *far* older than she claimed here, but as paranormals aged so slowly, and still held onto a lot of their dexterity and other powers, it didn't do anything to stop her.

"I don't have you down for an appointment until next week, Mrs Stein," Effie said, trying not to let her surprise show. This was still her job, even if people were trying to make it more complicated than it had to be for her.

"Daisy switched with me. Don't worry, I'm not breaking any rules."

"I highly doubt that," Effie muttered under her breath.

Mrs Stein chuckled as she hopped up onto the massage table. "A life without doing anything forbidden isn't worth living, dear. I'm sure you of all people know that. The faeries are notorious for their rules."

"They aren't that bad," Effie tried to protest, but her heart wasn't in it. She felt the same way the older woman did about the way the Faerie Council ran things. But until faeries of her generation sat on it, there was very little that could be done about it.

"If you keep telling yourself that, then it might be true," Mrs Stein quipped.

"Is there a reason you switched your appointments?" Effie asked, no longer feeling as if she had to be overly polite to the woman. She'd stuck her nose into Effie's private life, that gave her the right to be direct when it came to asking questions. "Have you been having some problems in the wing areas?"

"Oh, no. Of course not. I just sneak out at night and go for a little fly. No one notices."

Effie's eyes widened. She hoped Mrs Stein was a bird shifter, and not something much bigger that could fly. She didn't want to think about the papers if a dragon was spotted flying overhead.

"Is it something else? A tail maybe? I don't have much experience in that area, but at least you can tell me about it..." She picked up anti-bacterial wipe and started to thoroughly wipe down her hands. She'd washed them properly after her last patient, but she always wanted to err on the side of caution where possible.

Mrs Stein chuckled. "You young ones are always so eager to work, and never just to catch up. I wanted to check how our little MatchMater plan worked out." There was glee in the old woman's voice.

"Our?" Effie echoed as she dropped the wipe into the bin.

"Well, did you play along and use it? If you did, then I believe it is technically *our* plan, yes."

She shook her head, disbelieving what the old

woman was saying. She couldn't be serious, could she?

"So? Are you going to give me an update?" Mrs Stein swung her legs back and forth as she waited for Effie to say something.

The faery sighed. There was nothing for it. She'd have to tell the old woman *something*, and perhaps it might help her work out what she wanted to do about the whole situation. She suppressed a snort at that thought. She doubted an eight ball would be able to help her through this one.

"Your swipe matched with someone," she admitted. "But I haven't used the app other than that."

"Ahh. First time did the trick. You're one of the lucky ones. I've heard that for some people, it takes months and months." The sly smile on the woman's face told Effie all she needed to know. Somehow, this old woman had known what was going to happen. Perhaps she was a precog.

But no. That didn't make sense. She'd admitted to having wings, and precogs were witches, not shifters.

"I don't think I can go ahead with anything," Effie admitted, not knowing why she was revealing it to someone she barely knew.

"Of course you can. If the two of you matched,

then there must be some kind of connection," Mrs Stein pointed out.

"Well, I suppose there is, yes." She hated saying it out loud, but only because it reminded her of how impossible a relationship with Wendell would be. "But he isn't a faery, and that's the biggest problem."

"Hmm. That Council of yours should get its act together and realise it isn't the fifteen hundreds any more. They shouldn't be telling you all what to do."

"I thought that was the entire point of the Councils," Effie mused.

Mrs Stein laughed. "They're mostly there to keep the bad ones in check, not the lovely young things like you."

A blush spread over Effie's cheeks at that, and she ducked her head in order to hide it. "I still can't go against them," she pointed out. "They're my Council, and they can choose to expel me from the community if I break their rules."

"Ah, but don't they allow non-faery mates if you find them?" The knowing twinkle in the woman's eyes was hard to ignore. Well, actually, Mrs Stein as the complete package was impossible to ignore. Effie was surprised she hadn't heard more stories of the woman terrorising the staff and other residents. She seemed like the kind of woman who would get up to mischief at every turn.

"Well, yes. But that's only if we find them by accident. If we go looking, then we face expulsion."

"And that's where I come in."

"I don't understand." Effie shifted from side to side, trying to process what all of this meant. Should she be saying yes to Wendell's offer of a date?

She wanted to. Since the moment the question had left him, she'd been desperate to say yes, and she couldn't even explain why. But was it the sensible thing to do? If she was thrown out of the faery village, then she'd probably never see her family again. Or her friends. Would it be worth it? She wasn't so sure.

"Well, everything you've done has been after I meddled. Which means you never looked. All you did was answer a couple of messages and find your mate. All a coincidence..."

"Oh." She blinked a few times, processing what that meant. "So I can say yes to him?"

Despite being certain of what Mrs Stein was saying to her, she needed to hear it from the woman herself to make it real.

She chuckled. "That's still up to you, my dear. But the important thing, is that you can say yes if you want to."

CHAPTER NINE

WENDELL

HE STILL COULDN'T BELIEVE that she'd said yes. And that it had taken her less than a day to say it. And only another one for their date to actually come around. It was almost too good to believe, but he was trying desperately not to think about what would happen if she didn't show up. He wanted this to go well so badly.

And it would, he was certain of it. He'd done everything possible to try and make sure she'd be comfortable and not feel the pressure of a formal dinner date. Though maybe that was what she wanted anyway.

"Stop overthinking it all," he muttered to himself.

She was going to turn up. She had to. He couldn't stand the thought of any other outcome, no matter how hard he tried to deal with it.

"Wendell?"

Her voice travelled straight through him, along with the relief that she'd shown up after all.

"You came," he said lamely.

A soft smile spread over her face, lighting it up and only making her more beautiful to him than ever before.

"I said I would," she pointed out.

"That doesn't mean anything," he countered. "You could have changed your mind, or only said yes to keep me off your back, or..."

"Wendell..." She reached out and touched him on the arm.

The simple touch was too much for both of them, and they lapsed into silence while they stared at one another.

Eventually, she cleared her throat, breaking the spell between them. "I have to ask, why the aquarium?" She gestured to the building behind him. Not that she needed to. Anyone who lived even semi-locally knew what the aquarium looked like.

"I thought it'd be a nice non-formal date, as the idea freaked you out so much, I didn't want to make it worse." He paused for a moment, considering what he was suggesting. "I'm sorry, it was a terrible idea. We can go and do something else. Name it and we can..."

"The aquarium is good," she assured him. "I haven't been in ages, and I love to watch the penguins. Why don't we go and do that?"

"Are you sure?"

She nodded eagerly. "I promise, I'm sure. I think it's a great idea for a date."

He led her inside. Thankfully, there wasn't much of a queue, and the two of them were soon inside. Despite her comment about the penguins, she didn't rush to see them, but went through the rest of the aquarium first, commenting on the facts and the fish. Wendell quickly found himself watching Effie instead of the creatures. He knew he shouldn't, but the way her face lit up when she was watching and enjoying the way something moved was impossible to ignore. She was stunning.

No more than that. Ethereal. She was something far more than whatever paranormal being she was. Which was when he realised he still had no idea. It didn't matter though. It never would. She was his mate, no matter what she was, which meant he had the rest of his life to figure it out.

"That one's my favourite," she said, drawing his

attention to a penguin who kept falling over when he tried to get up the slope.

"Your favourite every time, or just this one?" he asked.

"That's a hard one," she admitted, amusement in her tone. "Sometimes, the ones that are exciting one time aren't doing anything other than sitting on an egg the next. That's a bit boring..."

"True. But do you get bored of your best friend when they're not doing anything interesting?" he asked.

"Good point. So by that logic, this one has always got to be my favourite. What's his name?"

Wendell pulled away from the glass to look at the list of penguins. "What colour band has he got around his leg?" he asked.

"Err...Green and yellow."

"Then it's not a he, it's a her. She's called Nessie."

"Like the Loch Ness Monster." she teased.

"I don't think *that* Nessie would like to be compared to a penguin," Wendell joked.

"No, I think dragons can get a bit prickly at times. I'm sure she wouldn't want to be thought of like that."

"Dragon?" he echoed.

"Mmhmm. It's common knowledge among the faeries that she's a dragon. Isn't it here?"

"No. And faery?"

"Are you going to carry on saying species at me as a question?" she quipped. "Because that could get old very fast."

"Sorry, I meant, you're a faery?"

"And how is that any better?" she asked, but the teasing nature of her words was clear in her eyes. "But yes, I'm a faery."

"But you don't have wings," he pointed out as he tried to process what that could mean without completely freaking out.

"And you don't have fangs right now, what's your point?" She turned back to the penguins as one jumped into the pool of water with a loud splash.

"They're retracted." The protest felt weak, even to his ears.

"Exactly. And so are mine."

"I didn't know faeries could do that," he admitted.

Another penguin jumped into the pool of water and started racing against the first one.

"Did you even know for sure that we existed?" Effie asked, keeping her tone light.

"No. But then, I could have mistaken you for an angel."

She snorted, an amused smile crossing her face. "That was terrible. Are you going to always subject me to pick up lines like that?"

He shrugged, enjoying how light it felt to be around her. It was so easy, even if she was teasing him. "I could try some fish themed ones instead, if you'd prefer."

"Hmm. Are there any fish themed ones?" She tapped her chin playfully as she considered.

Wendell thought hard. He shouldn't have suggested it when he didn't have any in mind.

"A shark ate my girlfriend, want to be my new one?" he said lamely.

Effie doubled over with laughter, clutching at her sides. "Seriously, that's what you're going with?"

"I was on the spot," he protested, beginning to laugh himself.

"Well, why don't we go see the sharks, and we can ask them for your ex-girlfriend back." She hooked her arm through his and drew him away from the penguins.

"I don't think they will. You're going to be stuck with me..." he teased.

"Let's just see about that."

"Should that be *sea* about that?" he countered.

She giggled. "You realise that joke only works if it's written down?"

"Then how did you understand what joke it was?" he returned smoothly. "Ah-ha, got you with that one."

"All right, yes you did," she admitted. "Shall we go see your ex? I mean, the sharks. Unless your ex is a shark shifter," she babbled.

"I can assure you, I've never even met a shark shifter."

"You don't know that for sure. Until five minutes ago, you didn't realise you'd met a faery either," she pointed out.

"I'm never going to win an argument with you around, am I?" Even as he asked, he realised he didn't care. Spending time with her was far more important than anything else, and he wasn't going to mess it up for anything.

CHAPTER TEN

EFFIE

HE'D SOMEHOW MANAGED to pull off the perfect date, which was impressive, given that she wouldn't have been able to put it together herself. But the aquarium followed by ice cream out in the sunshine by the estuary hit the spot. It was both charming, and romantic, with enough informality to put her at ease and stop her from overthinking too much.

Plus, she really did love the penguins.

She crunched on the last of her ice cream cone, glad she'd gotten the waffle one instead of the plain wafer. She'd hesitated, wondering if it made her greedy to do that, but decided she didn't care.

Lucky for her, Wendell ordered the same.

"You never told me what you did at the nursing home," he said.

She frowned. Hadn't she? Oh, that was right, all she'd said was that she wasn't a nurse. "You haven't told me what you do either," she pointed out.

"I'm a lawyer," he answered immediately.

Ah. Right. Which she could have worked out if she'd thought for longer than a moment about the legal advice pretence that Jim had concocted.

"I'm a masseuse," she said, realising there was no reason *not* to tell him. "Specialising in geriatrics."

"What got you into that?" he asked.

"Do you really want to know? Surely it's a boring subject to talk about on a date." She wasn't even sure if she wanted him to say yes or no. Did it matter what he thought of her job? A small part of her had to admit that it did. She wanted him to like all of her, especially what she did for a living.

"Of course. I want to know everything about you. Work is just the start. I know we've already talked about books, but I feel that subject still has a lot of talking time ahead of it. What about your favourite film though?"

She chuckled. "If you're not careful, you're going to end up firing twenty thousand questions at me and ending up with the answer to none."

"Sorry," he muttered. "I'm just excited. I've never

felt like this before. It sounds scary to say that out loud. Even scarier to think it, in some ways, but it's true. I can't believe this feeling is so new to me. It feels so comfortable, and yet so exciting at the same time."

She wasn't ready to tell him, but she felt the same way. It was impossible for her to not feel at ease with him, even though she barely knew him. And that in itself was exciting. None of the faery boys had ever made her feel this way while she was growing up.

"I got into it because I wanted to help people. When I have a patient, I use a tiny part of my magic to soothe away the ache of their bodies. I know that kind of thing is partly frowned upon, but I can't help it. I have to do it. How can I stand by and watch while people go through such pain?"

He nodded. "One of the reasons I got into law was because pro-bono work is such an expected part of the job. It's nice to have a company's resources and money behind you when you're facing a particularly tricky case, and it gets to help people at the same time. I couldn't do that as an individual, it wouldn't work."

"What do you specialise in?"

"Family law. Sometimes, it's horrible. Two people who used to love each other want a divorce and neither is really happy about it. Other times, it's satisfying to defend the downtrodden partner who someone is trying to take advantage of."

Her heart swelled at the idea of him helping people, it made her want him even more.

She tugged on his arm, bringing the two of them to a stop. She loved walking and talking like they had been, but for what she was about to do, she needed him to stay still.

"Is everything okay?" he asked, a puzzled expression knitting his brows together.

She nodded, then stepped closer to him.

His mouth formed a perfect o-shape as he realised what she had planned. His arm snaked around her waist. Wendell's gaze locked onto hers, seeking permission to pull her closer. He must have liked what he saw, as he did, bringing their bodies closer to one another than they ever had been. It was only then that Effie realised how much physical distance there'd been between the two of them.

Her wings fluttered in anticipation. She didn't think she'd ever needed to be kissed this badly in her life.

When his lips met hers, something snapped inside her, then settled into place. It was impossible to ignore the thrum of rightness which rested between them. This was more than just a kiss, and it was never going to be a one night thing. This was forever, she could feel it in every small movement of his mouth against hers.

He started to pull away, but she was having none of it, and pushed her body against his, and looping her arms around his neck. Wendell chuckled, the sound vibrating through their kiss, but he didn't try to stop it, for which she was grateful.

They finally broke apart, breathing heavily, and doing nothing more than looking at one another.

Which was when the magnitude of what had just happened sank in. He was her mate. There was no denying it now, even if there had been before. But what did that mean for her? Would she have to leave the faeries and everything she'd ever known behind in order to stay with him? Or was there a way she could work it out?

Mates. One word, on repeat around her mind. It was all she was going to be able to think about until everyone knew about it.

Her friends. The Council. Her Mum.

It was all too much. The shocking reality wasn't nearly as exciting as the hidden promise of passion.

"I'm sorry, I..."

She didn't finish her sentence, there was no way to without sounding awful. She pulled away from Wendell and flashed him one last apologetic smile before turning on her heels and running away.

"Effie!" he shouted after her, but she could tell he didn't follow. A small part of her was disappointed by that, but the rest was pleased that he knew how to give her space.

The thoughts in her head were a huge jumble of confused feelings and hope. She pushed them all to the side. She was only certain of two things.

Wendell was, without a doubt, her mate, and that this wasn't over yet.

CHAPTER ELEVEN

WENDELL

HE PASSED the living room as he pressed the call button. His heart felt as if it was about to leap out of his chest. He hated calling people like this, but it was Effie. Too much was riding on it to send another message via MatchMater that she could ignore. A call was more direct, and he liked that.

There was still a lot of confusion about what had happened. He thought their date had been going well. At least, he had until she'd run off straight after kissing him. Hopefully, it was something they could move past quickly. But if not, then he was determined to still find a way through whatever was happening.

"Hello," Effie said.

"You picked up," he responded in surprise.

"I did."

Silence grew between them, though it wasn't as uncomfortable as he feared it would be.

"I, err, wanted to check you were okay." He rubbed his free hand across the back of his neck, and finally stopped pacing. She'd answered. That was the first step on getting their mating back on the right track. There was a long way still to go, that was for sure, but talking was a start.

"I'm fine."

"But?" he prompted.

A loud sigh came down the line. "It's more complicated than you could possibly imagine."

"Try me." He tried to put as much earnestness as possible into his words. He needed her to know he was serious about it.

"I'm not supposed to spend much time out in the human realm," she said simply.

It didn't take a genius to work out that it was more than that, but he didn't push her. If he proved himself to be trustworthy, and that he respected her opinions, and choices, then perhaps she'd tell him what it was all about sooner rather than later. And if not, then that was her prerogative. So long as it didn't endanger anyone's life, it was fine by him.

"I'm sorry, that's hardly a worthy answer. I just don't want to talk about it now."

"That's okay," he promised. "If you don't want to talk about it, then you don't have to. But I'm here to listen if you need me to."

"Thank you."

"I take it from the fact you picked up the call that it wasn't something I did?" He wasn't sure why he asked it. Perhaps he shouldn't have. It would come across as a little insecure and potentially needy. He didn't care. The worst that could happen would be that she knew he cared, but she'd probably guessed that already. He'd been quite obvious about it.

"No," she whispered. "You were wonderful."

The words were faint, but he'd heard them, and pride welled up within him. He *wanted* to be that for her. And more.

"Would you like to come over tonight for dinner?" he asked.

This time, the silence was painful as he waited for her answer. But he didn't rush her. She clearly needed him to give her time. With their whole lives spread out in front, he could afford to take the time now.

"Maybe," she said.

Hope filled him. It wasn't a no, and at this stage, that was good. Whatever it was that was stopping her from coming into the human realm much, it couldn't have too much of a hold over her if she was going to consider coming.

"Okay. I'll text you the address."

"You're not angry that I haven't said yes?" she checked.

"Of course not. You get to decide what you do with yourself. I get no say in matters like that."

"Oh."

Huh, that must not have been the answer she'd been expecting from him.

Before he could think of something else to say, his front door slammed and his eyes widened. No one had the key to his flat. No. That was inaccurate. *He'd* never given anyone the key to his flat, which could only mean one person.

He had to get Effie off the phone now. He'd explain Cora to her later, but this was *not* how he wanted his mate to find out about the woman who was obsessed with him.

"I'm sorry, Effie, I have to go now," he said, hating himself for not already having told her about Cora. That would have made his life so much easier. But instead, he'd left it until now and almost got himself caught out. Which was ridiculous. Other than not telling Effie about Cora, he hadn't done anything wrong.

"Okay. I'll see you later," Effie said, sounding a little bit more certain than she had before. He wondered what that was about. Had she already made up her mind that she was coming after all? He hoped so, but he didn't want to push it

"I'll see you soon," he promised, then hung up.

Wendell readied himself for a conversation he'd had hundreds of times already, even though he knew it probably wouldn't work.

"Who were you talking to?" Cora demanded from the living room doorway.

"How did you get it?" he countered, even if he really knew the answer. He still needed her to admit it in order to change anything.

"Through the front door," Cora pointed out, attempting to purr. "You must have left it open, silly."

"I didn't," he responded flatly. "What are you doing here, Cora?"

"I came to see my mate. But he was on the phone to someone else. Who were you talking to?" She put her hands on her hips and attempted to look stern.

Wendell was sure the look worked on a lot of men, though probably not on those who had just found their mate. He sighed. Would the truth even get through to her? He supposed there was only one way to find out.

"If you must know, I was talking to my mate."

She blinked, stunned by the words she never expected. "That's impossible. You're mistaken. I'm your mate, and you know it. You can't deny the chemistry between us. The past. There's so much of it."

"I'm sorry, Cora," he said gently. "But it's true. I found my true mate, and it isn't you. I know this is going to hurt..."

"Oh, you do, do you?" she fumed. "You think it's going to hurt me? Why? Because I'm poor little Cora who doesn't know better?"

"What? No. Of course not. It's never nice to hear that you're not what you thought you were to someone," he said honestly while imaging how it would feel if Effie suddenly started insisting that the two of them weren't mates.

His heart went out to Cora, but that didn't stop the uncomfortable truth that she didn't want to admit. "You're not my mate, Cora. I'm sorry, but I've met her. I know it's going to be hard, but you're going to have to let this go. We can..."

Before he could suggest anything that might help Cora find someone of her own, she huffed and stormed from the room. The door slammed shut behind her. Wendell sighed, unsure whether or not he'd won that one. Somehow, he doubted he had.

CHAPTER TWELVE

EFFIE

SHE SET down her knife and fork, and looked across the table at Wendell. He was studying her intently, probably in an attempt to work out what she was going to do next. He was right to be wary, she hadn't actually worked it out herself. A small part of her couldn't even believe she was here. It hadn't been until she'd been half way to his flat that she'd even realised she was coming to see him.

"Dinner was lovely, thank you," she said, remembering her manners.

"You're welcome," he said. "I'm sorry it wasn't anything fancier. I didn't really plan to invite you around earlier. It just slipped out."

A small laugh bubbled up within her and escaped. "I didn't even know I was coming until I was here either. But I'm glad I did."

"I don't have anything in for dessert, but we could order some if you want. A new takeaway place has just opened up."

Was he trying to keep her here longer? She supposed it didn't matter what his intentions were, she wanted to stay regardless. She was enjoying his company, and wanted to get closer to him.

"I think I'm okay for now. But we could do something else?" she suggested, feeling somewhat emboldened by simply being here.

"We could queue up a film, or something?" he suggested.

Her heart swelled until it was at least double the size it should be. He was trying to ensure she was as comfortable as possible, and didn't feel like he wanted to take advantage of her. At least, that was her guess about what was going on. He had nothing to worry about, though. When she'd knocked on his front door, she'd done it with the full knowledge that she'd probably end up staying the night, and what that would mean. Both for her, and for their relationship.

After all, she wasn't fighting their mating bond. She accepted it was *very* real. The problem was simply a logistical one. There was a risk her people wouldn't accept them. And she had to decide how to break it to them while losing the least. That was all.

But for now, she was already away from the faery village, she may as well make the most of it.

"I was thinking that maybe you could take me on a tour of your flat..."

His eyes widened as he took in her meaning. "If you're sure."

"I am." She smiled at him, then rose to her feet slowly.

His gaze followed her every move, but she wasn't sure how to describe the emotion lurking in them. It wasn't lust, that was far too primitive of a word. It was like a combination of admiration, affection, and desire.

"Show me your room," she said. Nerves fluttered in her stomach, but they were good ones.

"Effie, we don't have to do this..."

"I want to," she assured him.

When he didn't respond quickly enough, she held out her hand. He took it, causing magic to zip up and down under her skin, as if it knew what was about to happen, and that it would be needed to seal the mating bond for good.

"We don't have to do this if you don't want to,"

Wendell said, his voice low and hoarse. Despite his words, he got to his feet. and came closer to her.

"I know, you don't have to keep saying that," she whispered. "I know what I want. I know what this will do. But I don't want to resist this any longer."

She closed the small gap between them and pressed her lips against his. He returned her kiss instantly, and pulled her closer with an arm around her waist. Their entwined hands let go of one another. Wendell tangled his now free hand in her hair, while she pressed hers against his chest.

Would he freak out if she started unbuttoning his shirt? He seemed a little wary about the whole thing, though she suspected he was simply nervous like she was.

"This will seal the bond, Effie," he whispered against her lips.

"I know."

"There's no going back."

A small laugh escaped her. "Because there's a chance of that if we don't?" she pointed out between kisses.

"You have a point there."

"So we might as well enjoy what we can of the ride." She began to tug at his shirt, though it didn't do anything to actually remove it from him.

"You're incorrigible."

"I try," she joked.

Wendell pulled back and cupped her cheek in his hand as he studied her with an intense gaze.

A blush rose to her cheeks. "What are you looking at?"

"How beautiful you are."

Her wings trilled beneath her back at the compliment. "That's one of your better pick up lines," she joked.

"Oh, then you're in for a treat when I reveal the next pick up..."

She was about to ask why he hadn't finished the phrase when he scooped her up into his arms. A giggle-like sound that she was reasonably certain she'd never made before in her life escaped from her. But she didn't care. Not only was this fun, but it made her feel more wanted than anything else in her entire life had.

"You're right, that is a good one." She reached out and booped his nose on a whim, causing a huge grin to break across his face.

"You wanted to see my room, right?" Wendell asked.

She nodded eagerly. "I suppose the rest of the tour can wait for the morning,." She sighed with fake exasperation, knowing he'd understand that she was joking.

He strode out of the kitchen and down a corridor. With every step he took, her anticipation grew. She'd dreamed about sealing her mating bond for a long time, and wondered how it would differ from the quick tumbles she'd experienced before. And now, she was going to find out.

"Are you going to bite me?" she asked suddenly.

Wendell paused with his back to the door of what she assumed was his bedroom.

"I can try not to, if you want. But I believe it sort of just happens the first time..."

She nodded. "That's okay then, just so I know what to expect."

"What do faeries do?" he asked, pushing through the door and revealing a surprisingly neat black and grey room.

"I don't know," she admitted. "But I look forward to finding out."

He chuckled. "Me too."

CHAPTER THIRTEEN

WENDELL

WENDELL HAS NEVER FELT SO content before in his very long life. Effie lay with her head on his chest, her hand stroking lazily up and down. He didn't even think she was aware of doing it.

"I'm surprised the dust isn't everywhere," he observed.

Effie laughed throatily, a reminder of what they'd been doing. "It's faerie dust, not sand," she pointed out.

"You're saying that like I'm supposed to know what it means."

"It's pure magic." She held up her hand and more of the sparkling dust that had covered her entire body at the same time as he'd bitten into her poured from it and onto his chest. It disappeared almost instantly, but not without leaving a pleasant tingling sensation on his skin.

"Handy."

"Very. It has healing properties too."

"It must be nice to be a faerie."

She snorted. "I wouldn't go that far," she muttered under her breath.

Wendell frowned, certain he was missing something. Being able to heal with her magic, and the other things she seemed to be able to do were all great as far as he was concerned, so why didn't she like it?

She sighed. "You know I said I wasn't supposed to leave the faery realm?"

"I think technically, you said you weren't supposed to come to the human one as much. But yes, I recall it." He didn't like where this was going.

"It is true, promise. We're encouraged not to leave unless we have to. A lot of faeries my age have jobs in the human realm because otherwise we get super bored."

"Ah, yes. Most vampires go through that phase. Some grow out of it, others carry on working. I think it depends on personality types."

She nodded, the movement only reminding him

of how closely they were lying, and how naked they were.

"Well, my parents are particularly fond of the old ways. The only reason they let me have my job is because they can't actually stop me as an adult. If I was under eighteen, then they would." She grimaced, but then carried on. "Well, part of the problem is that the Faerie Council encourages thinking like that. They go a lot further too."

An ominous emotion followed her words. Whatever else she had to say wasn't going to be good. "Why do I get the feeling I'm not going to like what you're going to tell me?"

"Oh, you won't like it in the slightest. It could make things difficult for us, and that's an understatement."

"Uh-oh." He shifted on the bed, but didn't pull away from her. He didn't want to.

"Technically, we're forbidden from searching for non-faerie mates."

He understood her words in theory, but it took a little longer than he wanted to admit for the meaning of them to break through. "So, you're trying to tell me that our mating is against the rules?"

"Yes and no." She bit her lip, clearly having no idea how attractive the motion was. "It's not forbidden for me to mate with you, it's forbidden for me to go looking for you. It's a nuance, and one we're going to have to play on."

"But you must have swiped me first on MatchMater..."

"Actually, I never swiped you at all." She laughed despite the seriousness of the conversation. "One of the old ladies did it for me. She's some kind of paranormal who has been meddling in mate lives. The fact that *you* were the one she swiped was pure coincidence."

"Do you really believe that?" he asked.

"That it's a coincidence?"

"Mmhmm."

"I suppose not, no. Mating is about fate, which means we were brought together. The way that happened is almost inconsequential when it comes down to it. We happened to be on at the same time."

"Is that what you're telling yourself in order to get around the Council saying no?" he teased.

Her expression grew serious. "It's not something we should joke about," she warned him. "The Council will take action if we go about it wrong. No one even knows what the punishment *is* for breaking the rules, no one in living memory has done it. But if we go about it carefully enough, then we might be able to get them to accept our mating without me losing my status as a faerie."

"I'm sorry you have to go through this." He kissed the top of her head.

She snuggled into him and let out a soft hum. "It's not your fault," she murmured. "Neither of us had a choice in this."

"That's true. And it's definitely too late to do anything to stop it now."

Effie looked up at him, something like desire in her eyes. "Then how about we do something that'll make it even later?"

"You're insatiable." But he loved it. And it would take her mind off the thoughts he could tell were still swirling around.

He'd never even realised the faeries existed, let alone that they were strict. When he thought about the way humans depicted them in paintings, they were so small and dainty, generally friendly too. But none of that matched up with what Effie was telling him.

Though it did match up with *her*. She was friendly and sweet and kind....

His thoughts were cut off the moment her lips met his again. He wrapped her up in his arms, determined to make them both forget about all the things they had to worry about. For now, they could simply enjoy being together, and learning how one another's bodies reacted to being touched. He'd thought about what having a mate would be like so many times, and yet this surpassed all of his wildest fantasies.

Effie was perfect. And she was his.

Just like he was hers. And he intended to spend the rest of their lives proving it to her, no matter what the Faerie Council had to say about it. There had to be a way to convince them Effie had done nothing wrong, he just had to find it.

CHAPTER FOURTEEN

EFFIE

THE SUN STREAMING through the window woke Effie. She stretched, enjoying the warmth against her bare skin, and the feel of Wendell's bedsheets below her. She'd certainly be spending more time at his. The bed was bigger than the one in her room for a start. Though the main factor would still be that it would be a disaster bringing a vampire back to the faery village. There could be a mob on their hands if they weren't careful.

The faint sounds of clattering came from the direction of the kitchen. Was he cooking again? She wasn't about to say no if he was, the food the night before had been delicious, as had other things.

It was better if she waited here until he came back, though. That way she could stay naked, and maybe entice him to come back to bed. On the other hand, she'd always wanted to walk around wearing nothing more than a man's shirt, perhaps this was the time to start.

She rolled onto her side and opened her eyes, searching the clothes strewn by the side of the bed.

"Aha." She snatched up the shirt Wendell had been wearing the night before, and slipped it on, carefully doing up enough of the buttons so it was closed, but not enough that it would cover her from him.

She sat up in bed, then froze as she noticed she wasn't alone. A woman sat on the end of the bed, wearing a tight dress that accentuated *everything*, in the right way. The woman crossed and uncrossed her legs.

"Can I help you?" Effie asked, confused and a little worried about what was going on. Who was this woman? And why was she in Wendell's bedroom?

The woman twisted and sighed, revealing an even more perfect face. A wave of self-consciousness swept over her. What business did she have in Wendell's bed when there was a woman like this around?

No. That wasn't fair. She was his mate. She had every right to be here.

The woman sighed again. "You had to ruin my fun, didn't you?"

"Your fun?" Effie's brows knitted together as she tried to work out what the woman could possibly mean. She hadn't done anything except spend the night with Wendell.

"You're stopping my mate from realising who he should be with," the woman said without a hint of malice. Instead, there was something akin to resignation in her voice.

"Your mate?" Did someone else live here? It seemed unlikely, there'd been no hints of anyone else in the other room she'd been in, though she supposed that didn't mean much when she'd spent most of her time fixated on the handsome vampire she'd come to see.

"Wendell. You know, tall, blond, likes to wear suits."

Effie's heart sank. "He's your mate?" Her heart sank. Why couldn't the floor open up and swallow her whole.

"Of course. Ever since we met twenty years ago."

"What?" The word slipped out before Effie could think about it.

"Which part are you struggling with?"

Shame seeped into every part of her body. What had she done? She'd been so convinced by the way she'd felt that she hadn't stopped to think if it was real, or if he'd been using her. She'd been too distracted by the stupid Faerie Council laws.

"I'm sorry, I didn't realise." She jumped out of bed and pulled on her clothes, the desire to get out of the flat and leave the whole evening far behind stronger than anything else.

The woman merely shrugged. "Don't be. If he didn't tell you about me, then you weren't to know. But you'd better be going now."

"I'm on my way out." Her shoes were by the front door, so she'd have to grab them as she passed, but she had everything else she'd come with, which was the main thing. "I'm sorry," she said again.

Without waiting for the other woman, she started to make her way through the flat and to the exit. To safety, even. Where no one would know what she'd done or who she'd come between.

"Effie?" Wendell asked.

She glanced over her shoulder to find him standing in the kitchen doorway, wearing an apron and holding a bowl of half whisked eggs.

"Is everything all right?"

"You know it isn't," she snapped.

He frowned, seeming genuinely confused. Did he

seriously think it was acceptable to tell her they were mates and not actually mean it? How *dare* he.

"No, I do...." he trailed off at the sound of door clicking further down the corridor. "Is someone else here?"

"You *know* who else is here," she hissed, feeling a lot braver than she'd expected.

Understanding and recognition dawned on his face. "Cora," he growled. "I'm going to..."

"Stop, there. I don't want to hear any more," she said, warring to keep the tears out of her voice. She shouldn't have been this foolish. She knew that.

"I can explain," Wendell promised.

But she didn't let him finish what he was saying. The risk of crying had become too much. She slipped through the front door and back out into the city so she could go home. Only once she was there would she be able to relax and let her emotions out. All of them.

"Effie! Please!" Wendell's voice called out behind her, but it could have been nothing more than her imagination playing tricks. Why would he run after her when he had a beautiful mate sat waiting for him.

Except, that wasn't necessarily the case, was it? Why had she taken the woman's word over his? If the woman, Cora, and Wendell *were* mates, then surely he wouldn't have been able to even look at her, never mind go any further?

She pushed the thought aside. It was a silly one. He'd known who the woman was without even seeing her. And what reason did this Cora have to lie anyway? There was none that Effie could find. Certainly none that had her walking in and out of Wendell's flat whenever she pleased.

No matter what Effie's gut instincts were telling her, she had to remember that she'd been had. Wendell was not the man she thought he was.

CHAPTER FIFTEEN

WENDELL

"WHAT THE HELL are you doing here?" The words came out harsher than Wendell had intended them to, but he was furious with her, and there was no hiding it.

"I came to see you," Cora said, calmly leaning back and spreading herself across his covers. "And shouldn't it be me asking the questions? You're the one who had another woman here."

"You're *not* my mate, Cora. I know you don't want to admit it, but it's true. I'm sorry. I really am. I'm not sure why you latched on to me. We spent one night together. One."

"One's all it takes," she pointed out, though he

could see the cracks starting to show. Perhaps this was the day he was finally going to manage to get through to her. He could only dream.

"And one is all it took for you to destroy my real mating bond," he seethed, before his anger started to ebb.

With a sigh, he dropped down onto the bed and cupped his face in hands as he tried to collect his thoughts.

"Look, I like you as a person, Cora, but you need to stop with the obsession. It isn't healthy for either of us. When I say I'm not your mate, it isn't just for me. It's for you too. You deserve someone who makes you feel the way Effie makes me feel. You should find that love too. You've spent twenty years of your life convinced it's me, what are you so scared of?"

He didn't think he'd ever seen Cora speechless, but now he was.

"I really am sorry," he said again. "I wish I could have been who you wanted me to. But we both know the mating bonds don't work like that."

"You really think she's the one?" Cora whispered. "Your mate?"

"I don't think it, Cora. I know it. With every fibre of my being. A moment without her is a moment wasted." And he'd ruined it. He should have told

Effie about Cora already, but there hadn't been the right time. And then she'd shown up. One thing was for certain, he was never keeping secrets from his mate ever again if this was going to be the result. It wasn't worth it. Especially as he hadn't intended this to become one in the way it had.

"Oh."

"You okay?" he asked her.

"That's not how I feel about you," she admitted. "I thought it was. I thought what we had was amazing and special and perfect. But it's not, is it?"

"No. I'm sorry. It isn't. But I'd like to think we can be friends?" he suggested.

"Even though I basically stalked you and then ran off your mate?" Guilt marred every word of what she was saying.

"Okay, maybe we can start slowly on the friends thing. And only when Effie's around too. If she ever forgives me." He didn't know what he was going to do about that. There had to be something that could convince her he was truly sorry and explain what was going on. It wasn't like he'd intended for this to happen.

"I'd like that, thank you," Cora said.

"And perhaps you could give me the copy of my key you made?" he suggested.

"Ah. Yes." She rummaged through her bag and handed him a perfect copy of his front door key.

"Maybe don't do this next time you think someone is your mate." He waved the key about to make his point.

"Got it. I hope you realise I'll be asking you for all the tips now," Cora promised.

He frowned. How had they gained such a strange relationship? He pushed the question aside. At the end of the day, it didn't matter. She was no longer going to be stalking his entire life, and as far as he was concerned, that was a good start to a potential friendship, though there was still a long way for them to go.

"And as for your mate, call her and explain. I'm sure she'll understand that I'm a little odd."

He chuckled. "That's what you're going for?"

"It's the official line," she reminded him.

"Got it. Now why don't you head home. Maybe even sign yourself up to MatchMater..."

"I don't think I'm ready yet," she admitted. "But I will soon."

He nodded. "But still go home."

"Let me know what happens with your mate. I'll let myself out." She got up from the bed and waved goodbye to him.

He stared after her for a moment, trying to work

out what had happened with the other vampire. It was almost anti-climatic given everything they'd been through together.

After giving himself a moment to process, he picked up his phone and dialled Effie's number.

Unsurprisingly, she didn't answer. What was he going to do about that? He had to talk to her and explain. He couldn't live his life without her, or they'd both end up miserable. Mates were meant to be together.

He hung up and tried again. At the fifth attempt, he knew he had no choice but to leave a voicemail, even if he hated them. There was nothing worse than the tape recorder icon hanging around at the top of his screen until he listened to the message, but if she wasn't going to pick up, then he had to.

"Please leave your message after the beep," the robotic voice said.

He took a deep breath. "Hi Effie, it's Wendell. Sorry, you probably know that already." He laughed nervously, hating how on edge he sounded. "I'm sorry about Cora. She's not what you think, I promise. She's believed we're mates since we met twenty years ago and er...spent the night together. Maybe that's not the best thing to admit to you while you're angry with me, but honesty is the only way we're going to be able to sort this out. Anyway, I've been trying to convince her we're not mates for years, and she finally seems to have understood this time. I'm so sorry I didn't tell you about it sooner, I promise I was going to. And Cora knows where she stands now. The only time I'll see her again is when we're together."

He thought over that last line, and regretted it. Oh well, it was too late now.

"Perhaps that isn't the best thing to say either, but I don't want to be the person who keeps secrets. Please forgive me. I need you, more than anything. I don't want to live without you."

Should he say more? He didn't think so, it was already a bad enough message without him complicating things further. With nothing else for it, he hung up, sending the message to Effie's inbox whether either of them were ready for it or not.

CHAPTER SIXTEEN

Effie

"*I don't want to live without you.*"

Wendell's words echoed around her head, along with his somewhat flimsy explanation. None of it really explained why Cora had felt the need to ruin Effie's perfect morning, and now she was left with a broken heart and a lot of questions.

The two were a bad combination on any day, but when her next patient was Mrs Stein, they were even worse. The woman had a sixth sense when it came to what was wrong with people, one that was only slightly disturbing, and Effie wasn't sure how to deal with it. She'd almost asked another masseuse to cover for her, but was smart enough to realise that wouldn't stop Mrs Stein. The older woman was the very definition of perseverance, and nothing as simple as a different service provider would stop her from interfering where she shouldn't.

Right on cue, the woman shuffled into the room, only becoming spritely once the door was closed and she knew no one but Effie was able to see her.

"Aren't you worried that we'll set up cameras in here or something, and show your secrets to the world?" Effie asked, her heart only half in it.

Mrs Stein chuckled and hopped up onto the table. "What secrets are they going to learn? That I can walk a bit faster than I claim to? There's no crime against that. Most of the nurses would only discover that they rarely have to help me, but I think they're grateful for that. It gives them more time for the poor old dears who need their help." She gave Effie a firm look. "Though I've been hearing reports of people feeling a lot better these days. Not as much joint pain, or a cough suddenly disappearing...."

"The doctor is very good at his job," Effie said.

Mrs Stein chuckled. "It's faerie magic, not incubus magic. I hope you don't think I'm oblivious to his secrets."

"I assume you know everyone's, it's safer that way," Effie mumbled.

"In any case, I'm sure if the humans in this place

knew you were the reason they were feeling better, then they'd want to say thank you. You improved a lot of lives, even if you didn't plan on it," she said.

Effie caught a small smile spreading over her face. "It's nothing more than what I started this job to do," she admitted. It was good to have someone like Mrs Stein out among the other residents. Knowing her magic was making a difference made everything worth it.

"But now we have the pleasantries out of the way, why don't you tell me what's bothering you, and we'll see what we can do about it?" she suggested, swinging her legs back and forth like she normally did.

Effie shrugged. "I don't think there's anything, really."

For a brief moment, she considered not telling the old woman anything about the situation. Then again, who else did she have to talk to? If anyone in the faery village learned she'd mated with a vampire, then there'd be hell to pay, and she didn't really have any friends on this side either.

Which was how she found everything coming out, in excruciating detail as Mrs Stein sat patiently and listened to each word, never butting in, not even with a wise crack or sarcastic comment. Effie even told her the part about Cora pretending to be

Wendell's mate. Well, if what he was saying was true.

A single tear rolled down her cheek as she finished by recounting Wendell's voice mail. The emotions of it all overtaking her in that moment. She wasn't sure she'd properly processed everything herself until she said it out loud.

"Hmm. I can see that's a tricky one. He's a fool for letting himself get into that situation in the first place."

Effie did a double take. Was the old woman taking Wendell's side in all of this? It hardly seemed fair, but then, none of this did.

"I think you should take him at his word," the old woman said. "You mentioned he sounded like he meant it when he was begging your forgiveness, so take him up on that. There's a reason you want to believe him."

She wanted to argue back, but then something came back to her. "There was a thought I had, when I was leaving his flat. Well, after I'd left, actually. But if Cora had been Wendell's mate, he wouldn't have been able to go on all the dates with me, right?" She crossed her fingers, hoping the old woman knew more about mating than she did. It was one of the many disadvantages of being a faery. They never taught any of the young ones anything useful. It was painful at times.

"You should trust your instincts," Mrs Stein said. "Once someone is mated, the only person they're interested in is their mate. That even applies to the fae. Your vampire is no different. If this Cora woman really was his mate, he'd never have downloaded MatchMater in the first place, he'd have had no need of it."

"Oh." She'd been right. It was reassuring to know that, but also kind of scary. If that was true, then she had nothing else to hide behind. "Do you think it would still be okay if I took another couple of days to process it all? I'm not sure how to talk to him again after I accused him of betraying me."

Mrs Stein nodded. "But don't wait too long. By the sounds of it, that man isn't the kind to wait around. He's going to try and convince you to take him back at every step of the way."

Effie laughed despite herself. "But if we're mates, aren't I always destined to end up with him?"

"Perhaps." The old woman nodded along with the word. "But I imagine you'd be fine if you chose to live away from one another. I've not seen my mate in a hundred years or so, and we're fine."

"Don't you miss him?" Effie asked.

"Of course. But let's just say we're watching over

different parts of the family. We have to be away from one another right now for the good of our clan." She smiled sadly. "You have a choice. I'm not saying that living away from your mate would be easy. It wouldn't be, at all. But you can choose to do it if you truly want to. Something to keep in mind."

A grateful smile graced Effie's face. "Thank you. I really appreciate your help."

Mrs Stein chuckled. "Of course you do, that's why I do it."

CHAPTER SEVENTEEN

WENDELL

THE VEIL to the faery village had been exactly where Mrs Stein had told him it would be, which was reassuring. He hadn't wanted to end up walking around the countryside endless looking for a way to get to Effie's home. The old woman had assured him that if he went to her, it would be worth it. He hoped she was right.

The village had been bustling until they noticed his approach. Faeries stared at him as he made his way to the centre of the square. He was lucky the village wasn't very big, it shouldn't be too difficult for him to find Effie in it, and they'd probably all know her name.

"I'm looking for Effie," he shouted.

The faeries looked between one another, some of them exchanging remarks.

"What are you doing here?" an older man asked.

"I've come to see Effie," Wendell replied, trying to keep his tone level and sure. He wasn't doing anything wrong by being here. Technically.

"Only faeries are allowed in the village," the man said.

"Actually, I believe that faeries and their mates are allowed here. I'm Effie's mate." He hoped the information Mrs Stein had given him was right.

More chatter came from that one.

"Wendell?"

He spun on his feet and turned to find Effie coming out of a house on the other side the square and sucked in a deep breath. Her wings were out, and it was the first time he'd seen them, and they were unlike anything he could have imagined. Intricate and translucent, then shimmered like the dust she created when she did magic. They suited her, and only added to the ethereal air she gave off.

"What are you doing here?" she asked.

"I came to prove myself to you. I brought a traditional offering for the Faerie Council in order to be accepted officially as your mate."

The old man before him stepped forward. "No

one has brought such an offering for years. What is it you're proposing has strong enough magic for us to accept a vampire into our community."

Wendell sucked in a deep breath and dug his hand into his pocket. When he pulled it out, he showed the man a sterling silver locket. "This belonged to my mother. She was given it by my Father the day they were officially mated. It includes locks of hair from each of my siblings while they were still babies, as well as me. I believe the offering of something that represents two kinds of true love is normally deemed to be sufficient. Especially when it is as old as this one."

He let the man take it from him, slightly saddened to see a possession his mother had treasured so much leave his care. But he knew she'd approve if she knew it would secure her son a future with the woman he loved.

"The offering is accepted by the Faerie Council on the condition that Euphemia confirms how the two of you met."

Effie flitted forward on her wings, gliding along the ground with ease. He couldn't believe he hadn't seen her fly yet.

"We crossed paths at my workplace," she said. "Wendell had come to meet one of the nurses to give her legal advice, and I was coming back from my lunch break and walked straight into him. There's a witness, a doctor who works there."

She was so smart. That was technically the first time they'd met, after all.

The old man nodded. "Very well, Euphemia, we accept your mate into our community. We expect him to uphold the faerie law where it applies, and you will be held responsible should he break any of them."

"Yes, Elder Santino." Effie bowed her head.

She turned to Wendell and grabbed hold of his hand, then pulled him back in the direction of her house.

"Euphemia?" he asked once they were away from the chattering faeries.

She grimaced. "My full name. You didn't really think my parents called me Effie when I was born, did you?"

He shrugged. "I hadn't given it any thought, the name suits you."

They ducked into a garden decked out with beautiful flowers and walkways. "No one will bother us here," she assured him.

"Good. I wanted to talk to you alone before all of that..."

She cut him off with a good-natured laugh. "That was never going to happen. You can't do anything around here without someone noticing, and then they all gather and do their thing. It's kind of creepy in a lot of ways, actually."

"Do we have to spend much time here?" he whispered.

She shook her head. "After we break it to my parents, I imagine we can spend most of our time at your flat."

"Or a bigger house," he suggested. "It depends when you want kids, or pets. Or if you want to work from home, or..."

"One thing at once," she suggested. "But does this mean I'm forgiven for running off without waiting to hear what you had to say about Cora?"

"Forgiven?" he echoed. "Why the blood would you need forgiving? I caused the problem by not telling you about her in the first place, I'm the one that needs forgiveness."

"We'd only been on two dates," she pointed out.

"Which is two more than we needed to know what we were together."

"True. So let's say we're even and both forgiven and move on?" she suggested.

"I like the sound of that."

She stepped closer. He slipped an arm around her waist, being careful not to catch her wings, though he'd want to touch them later and find out what they felt like. He imagined like silk.

All thought fled his mind as she pressed her lips against his. She melted into him, losing herself in their kiss. He let go too, taking everything she gave, and giving as much back. Her wings began to beat rapidly, and he didn't need to look to know they were sending faerie dust flying everywhere.

He was at peace. With Effie by his side, anything was possible.

* * *

Thank you for reading Forbidden Vampire Mate, and the MatchMater series. I hope you've enjoyed it. If you want more paranormal romance from me, then why not check out Bite Of The Past: http://books2read.com/biteofthepast
And if you want a glimpse into Mrs Stein's point of view, then you can in this scene from her point of view: https://dl.bookfunnel.com/hsj0i7azwv

AFTERWORD

Thank you so much for coming on the *MatchMater* experience with me - I hope you enjoyed it! I had so much fun writing all three of the stories and diving back into paranormal romance (and reminding myself how much I loved it!) While the *MatchMater* series is over, my paranormal romance isn't! I've been working on a second chance vampire romance called *Bite Of The Past* (and the prequel about the first chance!)

Some things in this series took me completely by surprise - Mrs Stein/Achilles' grandmother was one of those things! She took on a life of her own and became more than just a side character in book one. I loved being able to give her more of a role in this book. And she will be back in *Rising Aledwen*, the final book in the *Spring Fae Duology*!

It was slightly odd wrapping up *Forbidden Vampire Mate* during lockdown, while nursing homes are so off limits. I think that's one of the reasons I chose to set Effie and Wendell's first date at an aquarium. I'd already plotted it so that it would involve a light-hearted non-meal date, and I'm missing going to the local aquarium with it being closed and wanted to remember it in some way!

I hope everyone's staying safe! And I hope you're finding lots of awesome books to read!

Books in the Paranormal Council Universe

- **The Paranormal Council Series** (shifter romance, completed series)
- **The Fae Queen Of Winter Trilogy** (paranormal/fantasy)
- **Fated Seasons: Spring Duology** (paranormal/fantasy)
- **Thornheart Coven Series** (witch romance)
- **Return Of The Fae Series** (paranormal post-apocalyptic)
- **Paranormal Criminal Investigations Series** (urban fantasy mystery)
- **MatchMater Paranormal Dating App Series** (paranormal romance)
- **The Necromancer Council Trilogy** (urban fantasy)
- **Standalone Stories From the Paranormal Council Universe**

Books in the Obscure World

- **Ashryn Barker Trilogy** (urban fantasy, completed series)
- **Grimalkin Academy: Kittens Series** (paranormal academy, completed series)
- **Grimalkin Academy: Catacombs Trilogy** (paranormal academy, completed series)
- **City Of Blood Trilogy** (urban fantasy)
- **Grimalkin Academy: Stakes Trilogy** (paranormal academy)
- **The Harpy Bounty Hunter Trilogy** (urban fantasy)
- **Bite Of The Past** (paranormal romance)

Books in the Forgotten Gods World

- **Consorts of the Goddess Trilogy** (paranormal/mythology romance)
- **Forgotten Gods Series** (paranormal/mythology romance, completed series)

The Grimm World

- **Grimm Academy Series** (fairy tale academy)
- **Fate Of The Crown Duology** (Arthurian Academy)

- **Once Upon An Academy Series** (Fairy Tale Academy)

Other Series

- **Untold Tales Series** (urban fantasy fairy tales)
- **The Dragon Duels Trilogy** (urban fantasy dystopia)
- **ME Contemporary Standalones** (contemporary romance)
- **Standalones**
- **Seven Wardens**, co-written with Skye MacKinnon (paranormal/fantasy romance, completed series)
- **The Firehouse Feline**, co-written with Lacey Carter Andersen & L.A. Boruff (paranormal/urban fantasy romance)
- **Kingdom Of Fairytales Snow White**, co-written with J.A. Armitage (fantasy fairy tale)

Twin Souls Universe

- **Twin Souls Trilogy**, co-written with Arizona Tape (paranormal romance, completed series)

- **Dragon Soul Series**, co-written with Arizona Tape (paranormal romance, completed series)
- **The Renegade Dragons Trilogy**, co-written with Arizona Tape (paranormal romance, completed series)
- **The Vampire Detective Trilogy**, co-written with Arizona Tape (urban fantasy mystery, completed series)
- **Amethyst's Wand Shop Mysteries Series**, co-written with Arizona Tape (urban fantasy)

Mountain Shifters Universe

- **Valentine Pride Trilogy**, co-written with L.A. Boruff (paranormal shifter romance, completed series)
- **Magic and Metaphysics Academy Trilogy**, co-written with L.A. Boruff (paranormal academy, completed series)
- **Mountain Shifters Standalones**, co-written with L.A. Boruff (paranormal romance)

Audiobooks: www.authorlauragreenwood.co.uk/p/audio.html

ABOUT THE AUTHOR

Laura is a USA Today Bestselling Author of paranormal and fantasy romance. When she's not writing, she can be found drinking ridiculous amounts of tea, trying to resist French Macaroons, and watching the Pitch Perfect trilogy for the hundredth time (at least!)

FOLLOW THE AUTHOR

- Website: www.authorlauragreenwood. co.uk
- Mailing List: www. authorlauragreenwood.co.uk/p/mailing-list-sign-up.html
- Facebook Group: http://facebook.com/ groups/theparanormalcouncil
- Facebook Page: http:// facebook.com/authorlauragreenwood
- Bookbub: www.bookbub.com/authors/ laura-greenwood

- Instagram: www. instagram.com/authorlauragreenwood
- Twitter: www.twitter.com/lauramg_tdir

Printed in Great Britain
by Amazon